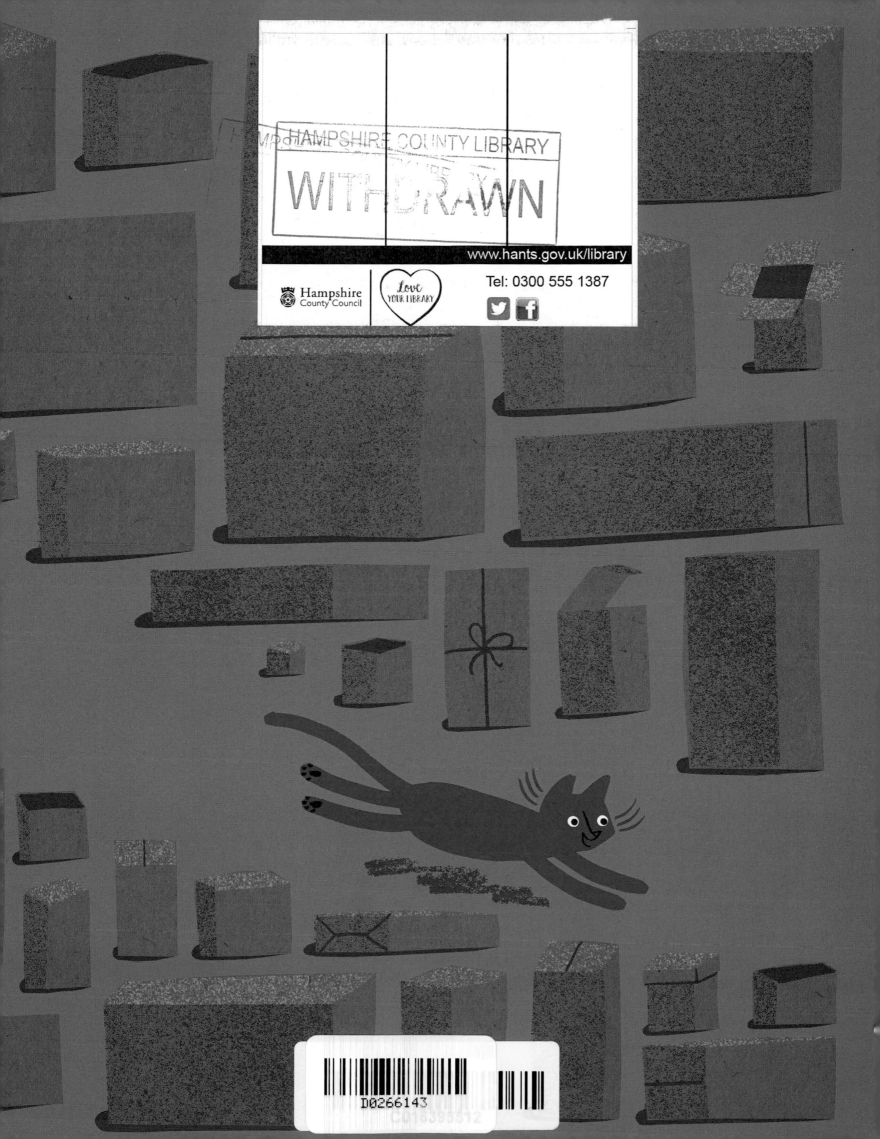

Dedicated to the Cats Protection League
for our lovely cat Bluebell — C. H.

To find out more about the Cats Protection League visit:
www.cats.org.uk

For Rita — E. U.

Bloomsbury Publishing, London, Oxford, New York, New Delhi and Sydney

First published in Great Britain in 2017 by Bloomsbury Publishing Plc
50 Bedford Square, London WC1B 3DP

www.bloomsbury.com

BLOOMSBURY is a registered trademark of Bloomsbury Publishing Plc

A CIP catalogue record for this book is available from the British Library

ISBN 978 1 4088 7277 2 (HB)
ISBN 978 1 4088 7278 9 (PB)
ISBN 978 1 4088 7276 5 (eBook)

All papers used by Bloomsbury Publishing are natural, recyclable products made
from wood grown in well managed forests. The manufacturing processes
conform to the environmental regulations of the country of origin

Printed in China by Leo Paper Products, Heshan, Guangdong

1 3 5 7 9 10 8 6 4 2

Written by

Caryl Hart

Illustrated by

Edward Underwood

BLOOMSBURY

LONDON OXFORD NEW YORK NEW DELHI SYDNEY

Big box

Little box

Cat box?

Flat box

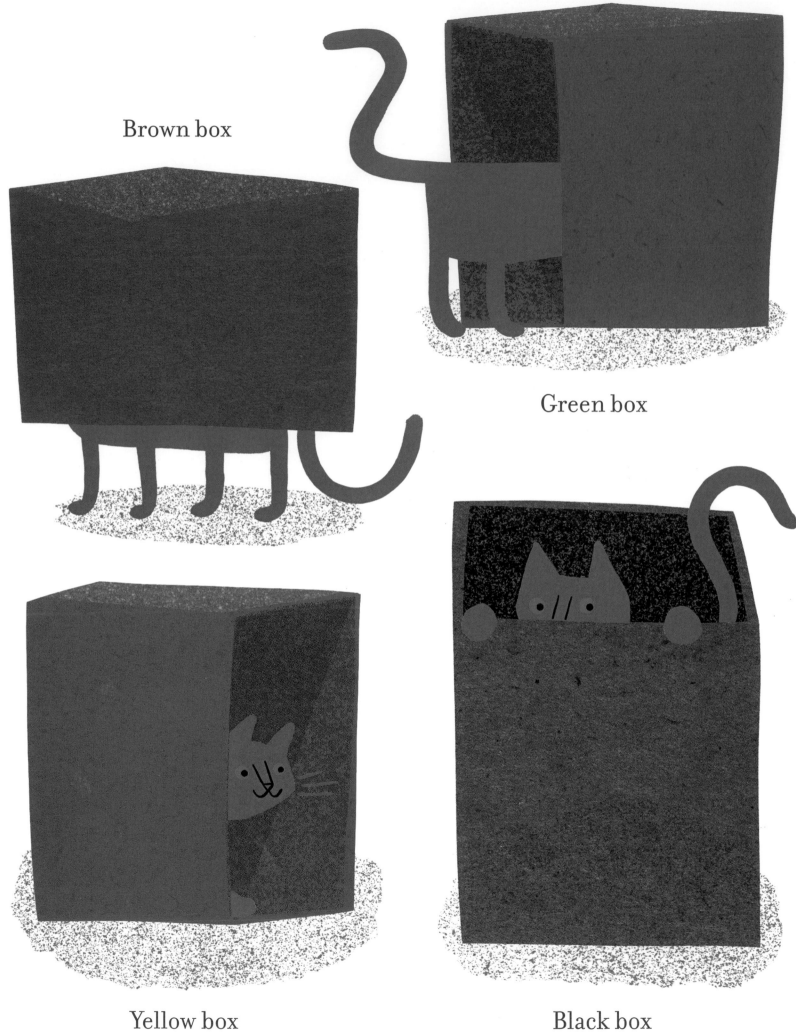

Brown box

Green box

Yellow box

Black box

Blue box

Red box

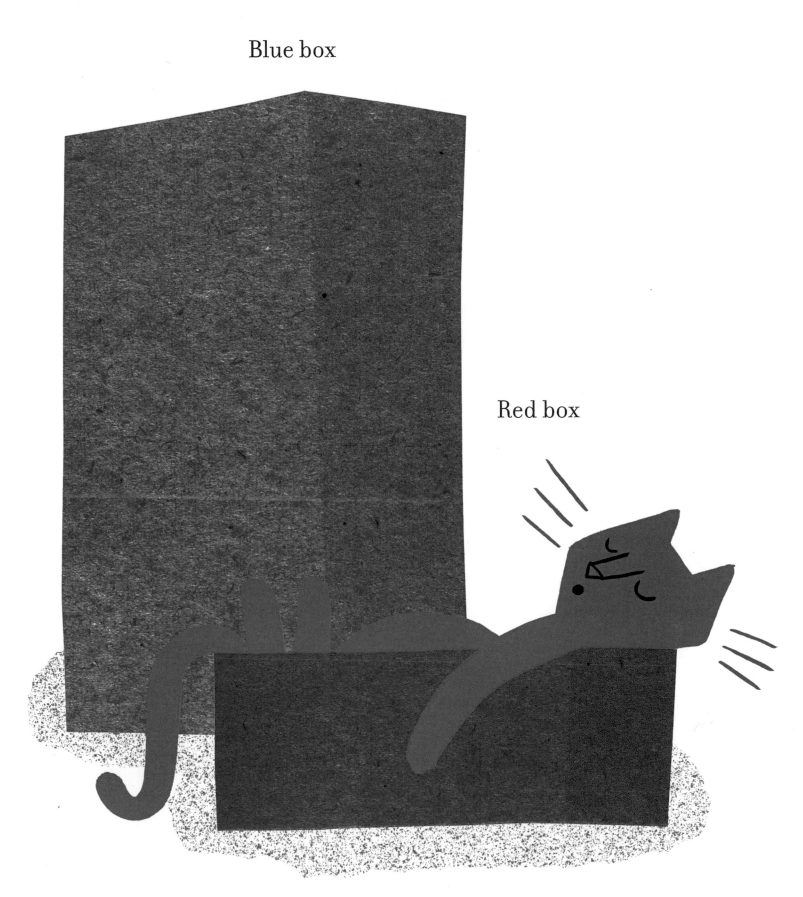

Hey! That's not a BED box!

My box

YOUR box

Snore box

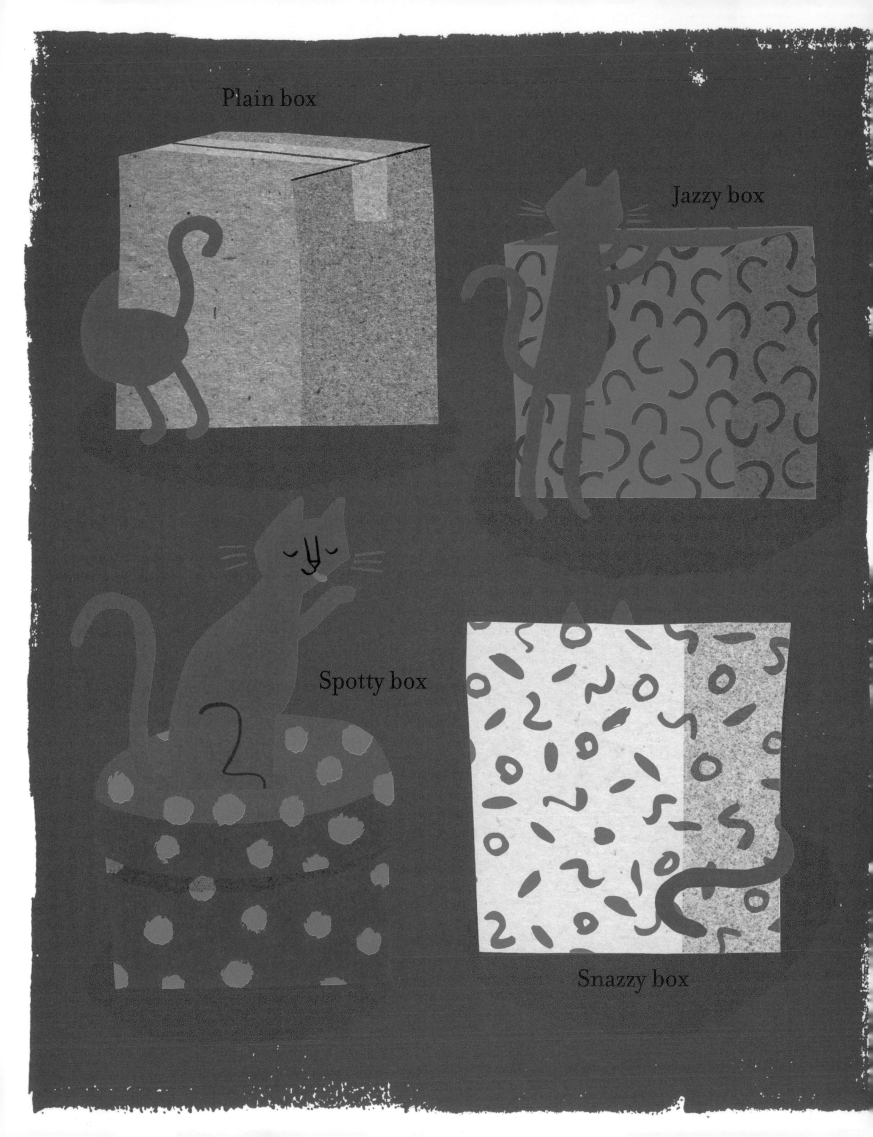

Plain box

Jazzy box

Spotty box

Snazzy box

Shoe box?

Hat box?

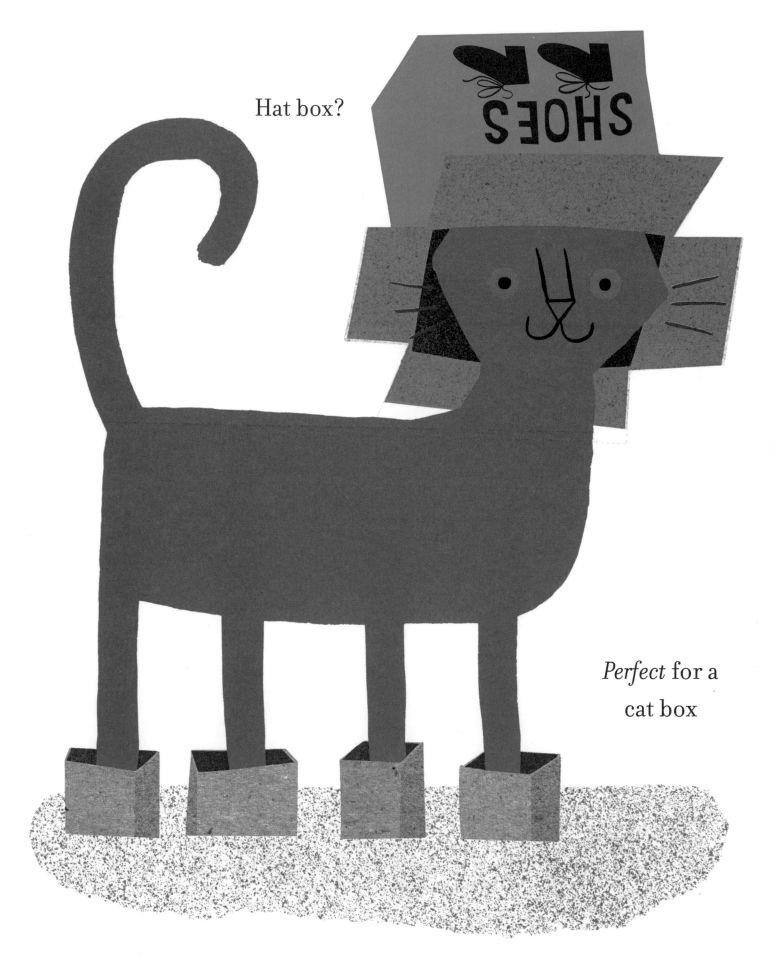

Perfect for a
cat box

Slippy box

Slidey box

Run away and hidey box

Box round

Box square

This one has a hole *right there!*

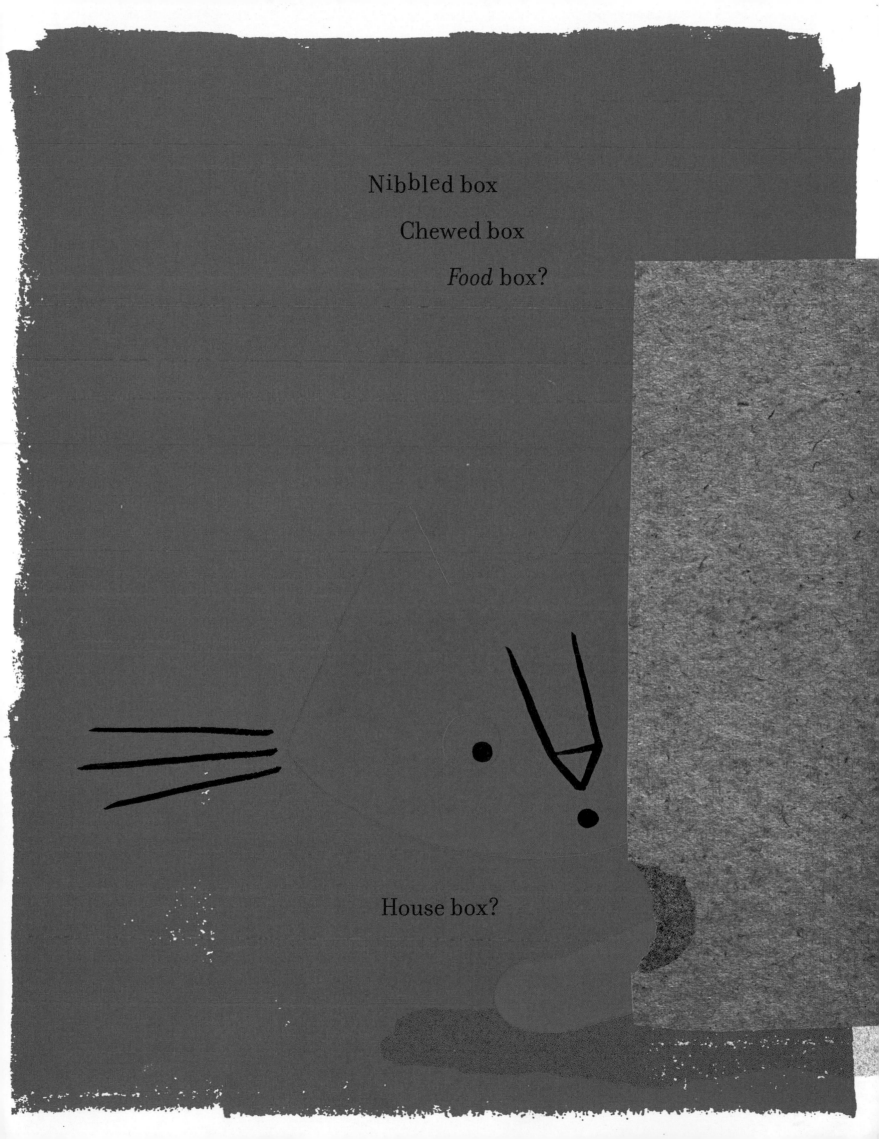

Nibbled box

Chewed box

Food box?

House box?

MOUSE BOX!

Cat peeks

Mouse squeaks

Scurry

Pounce

Chase

Bounce

Tickle

Purr

Warm fur

New friends

ENDS